Old Mother Hubbard and Her Dog

Old

handlettered by Cathy Altholz

First American Edition 1976. · Illustrations © 1974 by Ib Spang Olsen
Verses 3,5 and 10 copyright ©1975 by International Children's Book Service, ApS.
First Published by Rabén & Sjögren Bokforlag, Stockholm, 1974. All
Rights reserved. Published simultaneously in Canada by Longman
Canada, Limited. SBN:GB: 698-30600-7 SBN:TR: 698-20348-8
Library of Congress Catalog Card Number: 75-21967. 03209 PRINTED IN DENMARK

Mother Hubbard and Her Dog

original verses by Sarah Catherine Martin

translated from the Swedish version by Lennart Hellsing
by
Virginia Allen Jensen

drawings by
Ib Spang Olsen

COWARD, McCANN & GEOGHEGAN, INC.

NEW YORK

Old Mother
Hubbard
Went to the
cupboard
To fetch her poor do
a bone;

But when she got
there,
The cupboard was
bare
And so the poor dog had none.

She went to the baker's
To buy him some bread;

But when she came back,
The poor dog was dead.

She went to the graveyard
To dig him a grave;

But when she got back,
He wouldn't behave.

She went to the
fishmonger's
To buy him some
fish;

But when she came
back,
He was licking the
dish.

She went to the barber's
To buy him some shears;

But when she came back,
He was washing his ears.

She went to the
tailor's
To buy him a
coat;

But when she
came back,
He was riding
a goat.

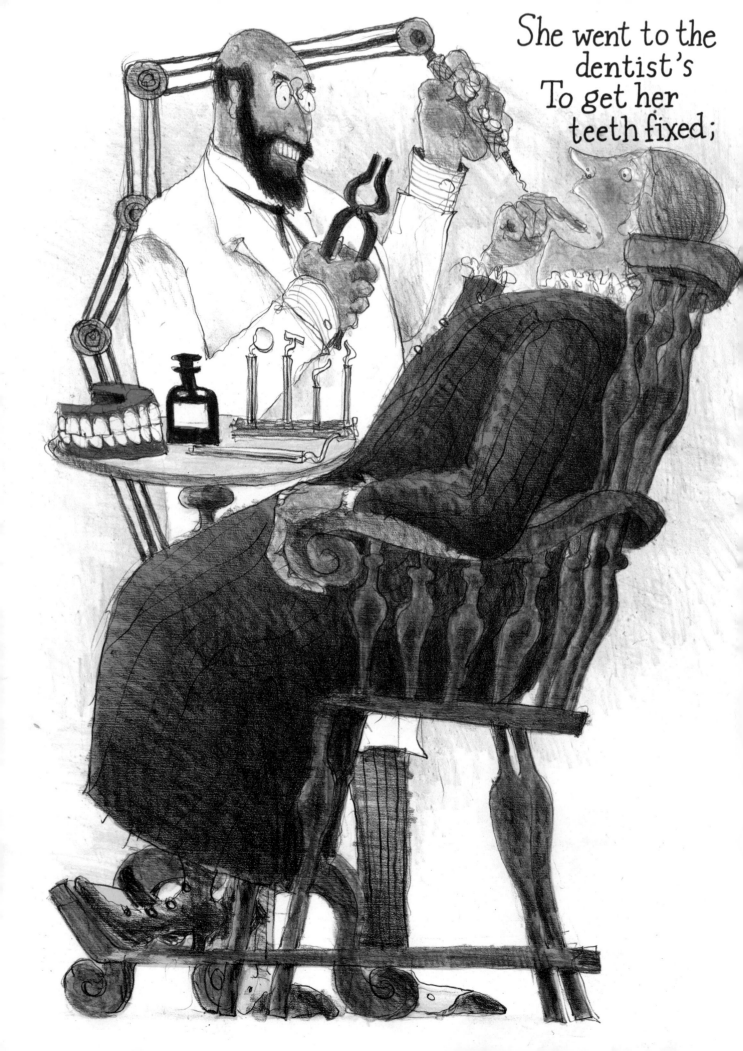

She went to the
dentist's
To get her
teeth fixed;

But when she
came back,
He was doing
some tricks.

She went to the hatter's
To buy him a hat;

But when she came back,
 He was feeding the cat.

She went to the
cobbler's
For shoes for his
feet;

But when she came
back,
He was making a
treat.

She went to the
tavern
For turkey and
snails;

But when she came back,
He was wearing his tails.

So Old Mother
Hubbard
Danced off in the
night

And didn't come
back
Until it was light.

About This Book

Nearly one hundred and seventy years ago, in 1804, Sarah Catherine Martin wrote a poem called *The Comic Adventures of Old Mother Hubbard and Her Dog*. The poem was published a year later by John Harris.

In all the years that have passed since Sarah Catherine Martin wrote the verses, English-speaking children have heard them and liked them. They have remembered them and later passed them on to their own children. In time, people stopped calling the poem by its long name and began calling it simply *Old Mother Hubbard*. You yourself probably know it by this name.

A Swedish poet, Lennart Hellsing, whose delightful nonsense verses everyone in Sweden knows, decided that Swedish children ought to know about Old Mother Hubbard, too. So he wrote the poem in Swedish and called it *Gamla Mor Lundgren (Old Mother Lundgren)*. Then he asked the Danish artist, Ib Spang Olsen, to illustrate the Swedish verses for a book.

Ib Spang Olsen liked the idea, and when he had drawn the pictures, he decided that Danish children ought to know about Old Mother Hubbard, too. So he wrote the poem in Danish and called it *Gamle fru Glad (Old Mrs. Happy)*.

When publishers in other countries saw the Swedish and Danish books, they liked them so much that they decided to have the poem translated into their own languages. Now children in many lands have this book about Old Mother Hubbard, but she has a different name in each language.

A problem came up when it was time to publish *Old Mother Hubbard* with these new pictures in England and the United States. Not all the old English verses fit the illustrations by Ib Spang Olsen. For example, one of the old English verses goes like this.

> She went to the cobbler's
> To buy him some shoes;
> But when she came back,
> He was reading the news.

In the new illustrations, Old Mother Hubbard goes to the cobbler's, all right, but when she gets back, the dog is making waffles, not reading the news. This is because the Swedish verse is not exactly like the English verse, for if Lennart Hellsing had written exactly the same words in Swedish, the verse would have been something like this.

> She went to the cobbler's
> To buy him some shoes;
> But when she came back,
> He was reading a magazine.

And there's no fun in that. So Lennart Hellsing wrote that Old Mother Lundgren went to the shoemaker's to buy some slippers *(toffler)* for the dog, and when she came back, the dog was making some waffles *(våfflor)*.

Well, "slippers" and "waffles" don't rhyme in English, and they don't fit the rhythm of the poem either. "Shoes" and "news" don't fit the picture. A new verse had to be made up; in fact, six new verses had to be made up for this book. See if you can figure out which ones they are. Then maybe you can make up some new verses yourself and draw new pictures for them, too.

Virginia Allen Jensen